Grace

FIRST
SECOND
THIRD

FOURTH
FIFTH

I Like to Read® books, created by award-winning picture book artists as well as talented newcomers, instill confidence and the joy of reading in new readers.

We want to hear every new reader say, "I like to read!"

Visit our website for flash cards, activities, and more about the series:
www.holidayhouse.com/ILiketoRead
#ILTR

This book has been tested by an educational expert and determined to be a guided reading level E.

KATE PARKINSON

HOLIDAY HOUSE • NEW YORK

Grace wanted to dance.

She tried.

And she tried.

And she tried.

“Give up, Grace,” the other girls said.

Grace was sad.

She made a picture
and felt better.

Grace made many pictures.
Then she had an idea.

The other girls loved what Grace made.

Grace felt great.

So she kept making pictures.

She kept dancing too.

To my dad, with love; my mum, whose light shines on in me;
and with a special thanks to Ted and Betsy Lewin
for their inspiration and encouragement

Printed and Bound in August 2018 at Toppan Leefung, DongGuan City, China.
The artwork was created with pen and ink and Photoshop.
www.holidayhouse.com
5 7 9 10 8 6 4

Library of Congress Cataloging-in-Publication Data
Parkinson, Kate, author, illustrator.
Grace / by Kate Parkinson. — First edition.
pages cm. — (I like to read)
Summary: When the other girls discourage Grace from dancing,
she draws pictures to make herself feel better and succeeds
in a surprising way.
ISBN 978-0-8234-3207-3 (hardcover)
[1. Ability—Fiction. 2. Dance—Fiction. 3. Drawing—Fiction.] I. Title.
PZ7.P23933Gr 2015
[E]—dc23
2014006417

ISBN 978-0-8234-3317-9 (paperback)

You will like these too!

Come Back, Ben by Ann Hassett and John Hassett
A *Kirkus Reviews* Best Book

Dinosaurs Don't, Dinosaurs Do by Steve Björkman
A Notable Social Studies Trade Book for Young People

Fish Had a Wish by Michael Garland
A *Kirkus Reviews* Best Book

The Fly Flew In by David Catrow
Maryland Blue Crab Young Reader Award Winner

Late Nate in a Race by Emily Arnold McCully
A Bank Street College Best Children's Book of the Year

Look! by Ted Lewin
The Correll Book Award for Excellence
in Early Childhood Informational Text

Me Too! by Valeri Gorbachev
A Bank Street College Best Children's Book of the Year

Mice on Ice by Rebecca Emberley and Ed Emberley
An IRA/CBC Children's Choice

Pig Has a Plan by Ethan Long
An IRA/CBC Children's Choice

See Me Dig by Paul Meisel
A *Kirkus Reviews* Best Book

See Me Run by Paul Meisel
A Theodor Seuss Geisel Award Honor Book
An ALA Notable Children's Book

You Can Do It! by Betsy Lewin
A Bank Street College Outstanding Children's Book

See more I Like to Read® books.
Go to www.holidayhouse.com/ILiketoRead

I Like to Read® Books in Paperback
You will like all of them!

Bad Dog by David McPhail
The Big Fib by Tim Hamilton
Boy, Bird, and Dog by David McPhail
Can You See Me? by Ted Lewin
Car Goes Far by Michael Garland
Come Back, Ben by Ann Hassett and John Hassett
The Cowboy by Hildegard Müller
Dinosaurs Don't, Dinosaurs Do by Steve Björkman
Ed and Kip by Kay Chorao
The End of the Rainbow by Liza Donnelly
Fireman Fred by Lynn Rowe Reed
Fish Had a Wish by Michael Garland
The Fly Flew In by David Catrow
Good Night, Knight by Betsy Lewin
Grace by Kate Parkinson
Happy Cat by Steve Henry
I Have a Garden by Bob Barner
I Said, "Bed!" by Bruce Degen
I Will Try by Marilyn Janovitz
Late Nate in a Race by Emily Arnold McCully
The Lion and the Mice by Rebecca Emberley and Ed Emberley
Little Ducks Go by Emily Arnold McCully
Look! by Ted Lewin
Look Out, Mouse! by Steve Björkman
Me Too! by Valeri Gorbachev
Mice on Ice by Rebecca Emberley and Ed Emberley
Pete Won't Eat by Emily Arnold McCully
Pig Has a Plan by Ethan Long
Ping Wants to Play by Adam Gudeon
Sam and the Big Kids by Emily Arnold McCully
See Me Dig by Paul Meisel
See Me Run by Paul Meisel
A Theodor Seuss Geisel Award Honor Book
Sick Day by David McPhail
3, 2, 1, Go! by Emily Arnold McCully
What Am I? Where Am I? by Ted Lewin
You Can Do It! by Betsy Lewin